This
Judy Moody
Mood Journal
is the property of:

Claire

- paste your picture here -

I started writing in my journal on 12.11.11 .

My favourite page is _____.

If you read my journal, you'll put me in a cool mood!

This product is intended for use by children over six years of age.

First published 2003 by Walker Books Ltd
87 Vauxhall Walk, London SE11 5HJ

2 4 6 8 10 9 7 5 3

This book has been typeset in Stone Informal and Judy Moody

Printed in the United States of America

Spinner on cover provided by Innovative Mold Inc.;
Faribult, MN; www.PrototypeMold.com

ISBN 0-7445-9863-X

www.walkerbooks.co.uk

Meet Judy Moody!

Judy Moody is always in a mood.
Good moods, bad moods and mad-face moods.
Goofy, grumpy, glad moods.

Here's what puts Judy in a top-of-the-world mood:

- tiger-striped pyjamas
- her best friend, Rocky (who likes magic tricks)
- her friend Frank Pearl (who likes to eat paste)
- cool things to collect, like Band-Aids and pizza tables
- recycling
- Screamin' Mimi's Chocolate Mud ice cream

Here's what puts Judy in a pencil-snapping mood:

- her little brother, Stink (most of the time)
- Jessica Finch, know-it-all spelling bee champ, aka Queen Bee
- piano-playing chickens
- all-boy parties
- maths-test Mondays
- mood rings that turn black for burnt-toast bad moods

**This Judy Moody journal is perfect
for writing about what puts *you* in a mood!
Just turn the page to get started . . .**

can't read
this ⟶

Judy was in a
positively purple,
on-top-of-spaghetti-and-the-world mood.

The random Storie

12/12/11

Once a pon a time there was a cow called HARRY Potter he know a girl called hemire and so know a boy called Ron they were magit Then had wards they had a evil nemices called VOldemort he was maed to the were fighting him a voldemort LOST The End

What Mood Are You In . . .

first thing in the morning?

_____

_____

_____

_____

_____

on the first day of school?

_____

_____

_____

_____

_____

_____

when your brother or sister plays a trick on you?

_____

_____

_____

_____

_____

_____

_____

on your birthday?

_____

_____

_____

_____

_____

_____

I think   teacher thinks
:   :

_____

Maths

$2 \times 0 = 0$

$2 \times 1 = 2$ ✓
                          well done.

$2 \times 2 = 4$ zoe. next time tell

$2 \times 3 = 6$ Abigail off if

$2 \times 4 = 8$ she marks your

$2 \times 5 = 10$ jotter. ☺

$2 \times 6 = 12$

$2 \times 7 = 14$

$2 \times 8 = 16$

$2 \times 9 = 18$

$2 \times 10 = 20$ ✓

really neat!

better than las week!

Practising with my left
hand.

pigs Love Claire

Right Hand

pigs Love Claire

Judy was in a mood. Not a good mood.
A bad mood. A mad-face mood.

Stink Stinks

Stink

- Judy's younger brother (aka "bother")
- Loves his pet, Toady
- Star of the Moody Hall of Fame

Do you have a nickname like Stink does?

yes it is   chigaboo

If you do, what is it?

chigaboo

How do you think Stink got his nickname?

becouse he is really stinky

"Judy Moody" rhymes. Can you make your name rhyme?

If anybody could put Judy in a bad mood, Stink could.
The baddest.

"Bothers" & Sisters

Do you have any brothers or sisters? What are their names and ages?

No

_____

Do they ever bug you? How?

No

_____

What's the funniest-trick-ever you played on your brother or sister?

_____

_____

_____

_____

GROUCHY
pencils – for
completely
impossible
moods.

19. 11. 12

spelling

Doll ✓

pull ✓

coul ✓

DOll ✓

pull ✓

cool ✓

Well done could of been neter

HELP!
Even My Pencil's in a Mood!

Design your own Grouchy pencil here:

———————————————

———————————————————————————————

———————————————————————————————

———————————————————————————————

———————————————————————————————

———————————————————————————————

———————————————————————————————

———————————————————————————————

———————————————————————————————

———————————————————————————————

If Stink were a volcano,
he would have spewed lava.

12.11.11

Fire register

Chloe						
Zoe						
Abigail						
Hollie						
molly						
Taylor						
Caitlin						
Rachael						

12.11.11

Monday
Spelling

-ow ham   rex _ed
    blow   cooked
  follow   looked
  below   invented

Best Friends

Judy Moody's Best Friends

Rocky

Frank

- Likes magic tricks
- Owns rubber hand
- Makes Judy laugh

- Eats paste
- Collects stuff
- Always there when you need him

Pick a friend. Make a list of stuff you like about him or her:

- _____
- _____
- _____
- _____
- _____
- _____

Draw a picture of your friend:

(name)

What really bugs you about your friend?

_____

_____

_____

_____

_____

_____

Write about a funny thing you did with your friend.

_____

_____

_____

_____

_____

"Same-same!" said Judy and Rocky, slapping hands together twice in a high-five, the way they always had when they did something exactly alike.

_____

_____

_____

_____

_____

_____

_____

_____

_____

_____

_____

_____

Ever since they had danced the Maypole together in kindergarten, Frank would not leave Judy alone.

Best-Ever Stuff in the World

Lucky stone

pizza table ↑

5 pink pebbles

bubblegum forbie

blue lego

What's your favourite...

Colour:
(Red, vermilion, pond-scum green?)

Blue

Game:
(Operation? Concentration?)

twister

Book:
(Judy Moody Goes to Antarctica?
The "S" encyclopedia?)

James and
Giant peach

Food:
(Jell-O? Pop Rocks?
Screamin' Mimi's ice cream?)

sweet

Thing to collect:
(Pizza tables? Scabs?
Barbie doll heads?)

Movie:
(Godzilla Meets Jaws?)

Judy licked her
Rainforest Mist
scoop on top of
Chocolate Mud,
her favourite.
She was in her
best Judy Moody
mood ever.

Funniest Thing Ever

Write about the funniest thing that ever happened to you.

_____

_____

_____

_____

_____

_____

Worst Thing Ever

Write about the worst thing that ever happened to you.

_____

_____

_____

Yuckiest Thing Ever

Write about the yuckiest thing that ever happened to you.

_____

_____

_____

_____

_____

_____

_____

She, Judy Moody, was definitely the one and only girl. . . Frank Pearl's all-boy party had to be THE WORST THING THAT EVER HAPPENED to her.

Favourite Pets

Mouse

- Judy's cat
- Fond of bananas
- Makes toast

Toady

- Stink's toad
- Toad Pee Club mascot
- Was lost and found!

Do you have any pets?

yes

What are their names?

Figo

Write about a funny trick your pet can do.

If you could have any pet you wished for, what would it be?

dog

What would you name your new pet?

figo

Judy scooped up her cat and kissed him on the nose: "*Mww, mww, mww.* You are the best, most wonderful cat in the whole wide world with tuna fish on top."

Make a ME Collage!

A ME collage is a collage all about YOU!
Paste stuff (like pictures from magazines, photos, ticket stubs) here:
(BLUCK! No eating the paste!)

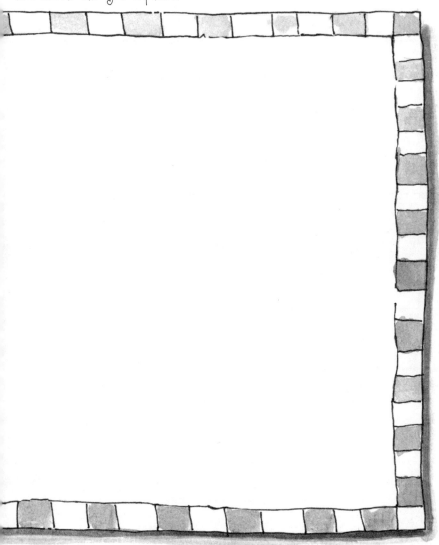

Judy tried to look like a person who would grow up to be a doctor and make the world a better place. A person who could turn a bad mood right around.

THE Toad Pee Club

Are you in a club?

<u>yes</u>

The name of Judy's club is the Toad Pee Club. What's the name of your club?

<u>Disco dancing</u>

There was something warm and wet on his hand. Judy Moody and Rocky fell down laughing.

"Am I in the club yet?" asked Stink.

"Yes! Yes! Yes!" said Judy and Rocky.

"The Toad Pee Club!"

"Yippee!" cried Stink.

Emergency meeting of the Toad Pee Club today! Pass this to Rocky —J.M.

What do you do in your club?

dance

Write about a club you'd like to be in.

Disco dancing

3.4.12
Spelling _y

Mummy

-y

Puppy

lolly

Spelling   Sentinsas
1. I love Mummy
2. I likt a lolly pop
3. I have a puppy

_____

Judy grabbed Mouse. "Mouse could be our new mascot!"
"The Mouse Pee Club? I don't think so," said Stink.
"See? If it wasn't for Toady, there wouldn't even be
a Toad Pee Club."

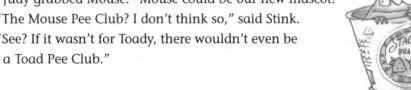

Knock-Knocks

Write your own Knock-Knock Joke

Knock, knock.

Who's there?

Knock Knock Who's there?

docter   who?

you just siad it   !

"Go away," said Judy.
"Knock, knock!" said Stink.
"Who's there?" said Judy.
"I, Stink," said Stink.
"I Stink who?"
"I stink you should let me
in your room," said Stink,
letting himself in anyway.

Claire

neat writing not
wanting to do trace a
shape

_____

_____

_____

_____

_____

_____

_____

_____

_____

_____

"OK. OK. I cannot
tell a lie. I coughed
a cherry pit at Stink."

Red in the Face

What makes you turn fire-engine red?

_____

_____

_____

_____

_____

Write about your most embarrassing moment.

_____

_____

_____

_____

_____

_____

All eyes were on Judy. She turned fire-engine red.
Hide-your-face-in-your-hands red. Big-fat-dictionary red.

Save the World!

How would YOU save the world?

_____

_____

_____

_____

_____

_____

_____

_____

_____

In a World-Saving Mood

One person! If all it took was one person,
then she, Judy Moody, could save the world!

_____

Saving the world was not going so well. . .
So far, Judy had only saved four banana
peels, a lunch bag and a toad.

Judy Moody
is

Batty for Band-Aids!

Design your own Band-Aid:

_____

_____

_____

_____

_____

_____

_____

_____

_____

_____

Dear Mr Moody,

Congratulations! You are a winner in the Crazy Strips Design Your Own Bandage Contest! Your design, Batty for Band-Aids, will be a featured Crazy Strip of the Month for October.

M. L. Donovan
CRAZY STRIPS C.E.O.

Stink had his own Crazy Strip! Her very own batty little brother was now as famous as Josephine Dickson, Inventor of the Adhesive Bandage.

My Room

Judy Moody's room has:

- A jelly bean collection
- Bunk beds
- Sock Monkey
- Doctor Kit
- Protect the Planet poster
- Mouse

My room has:

posters

TV

Book case

My dream room has:

pony Wall papper

Drawin Tabel

pink TV

Draw a picture of your dream room:

"Green means green with envy.
Green means you wish you were me."
—Judy Moody

Pizza, Zip, Zap . . .

Are you in a Spelling mood?

How many new words can you make from

Gino's Extra-Cheese Pizza?

List them here:

in

to

Exit

_____

_____

_____

_____

_____

_____

_____

Judy could not help thinking how stupendous it would feel to be able to spell better than *meatloaf* and be the Queen Bee and wear a tiara.

Tiger-Striped Pyjamas!

Did you ever wear pyjamas to school?

_____ No _____

If so, why?

_____

_____

What would you do if you went to school in your pyjamas by mistake?

_____

_____

_____

_____

_____

Moody Hall of Fame

Stink made his own Hall of Fame on the refrigerator.

In the Hall of Fame was:

- his report card
- a self-portrait that made him look like a monkey
- a photo of himself in his flag costume, from the time he went to Washington, DC, without Judy

If you could hang things on your refrigerator Hall of Fame, what would they be?

- _____
- _____
- _____
- _____

Famous!

Think of ways you might get your picture in the paper:

_____

_____

_____

_____

Write about getting your picture in the paper:

_____

_____

Draw a picture of yourself, in the newspaper:

For
the first
time in
a long
time, the
once Judy
Muddy
felt more
famous
than an
elbow.

The Future You!

Predict your own future!
What would you like to be when you grow up?

___be a vet___

_____

_____

_____

_____

Where would you like to live?

___in a house___

_____

_____

_____

_____

Is there anyone you admire? Would you like to be like them?
Why or why not?

_____

_____

_____

_____

_____

_____

_____

_____

_____

_____

_____

_____

_____

The future was
out there, waiting.
And there was
one more thing
Judy knew for
sure and absolute
positive – there
would be many
more moods to
come.

Groups   Groups

Jessie   spelling

○   Jessies

    Maths

    ○

    reading

    cats

    writing

    blue

    Talking partner

    caitlen

Groups

Spelling

ham: Zoe + abigail + Taylor + Rachael

rex: chloe + caitlin + hollie + Molly

Writing

Want to know more about Judy Moody? Read her books!

Judy Moody
Judy doesn't have high hopes for third grade, but when Mr Todd assigns a very special class project, she really gets a chance to express herself!

Judy Moody Gets Famous!
When Judy sets off in pursuit of fame, watch out!

Judy Moody Saves the World!
Judy's in a mood to whip the planet into shape!

Judy Moody Predicts the Future
A mood ring's Extra Special Powers have put Judy in a predicting mood.